MW00902955
A
KILLER
SECRET
JESSICA ALLEN

ISBN 978-1-0980-9980-0 (paperback)
ISBN 978-1-0980-9981-7 (digital)

Copyright © 2021 by Jessica Allen

All rights reserved. No part of this publication may be reproduced, distributed, or transmitted in any form or by any means, including photocopying, recording, or other electronic or mechanical methods without the prior written permission of the publisher. For permission requests, solicit the publisher via the address below.

Christian Faith Publishing, Inc.
832 Park Avenue
Meadville, PA 16335
www.christianfaithpublishing.com

Printed in the United States of America

CONTENTS

ACKNOWLEDGMENTS

FOR THIS BOOK, THE previous, and all the books to come, I want to thank Dr. Sean Martin for always encouraging me and challenging me to write. I am so thankful for all of the professors I had at Duquesne University and Point Park University for always pushing me to do my best and to look for new challenges to conquer!

A KILLER SECRET

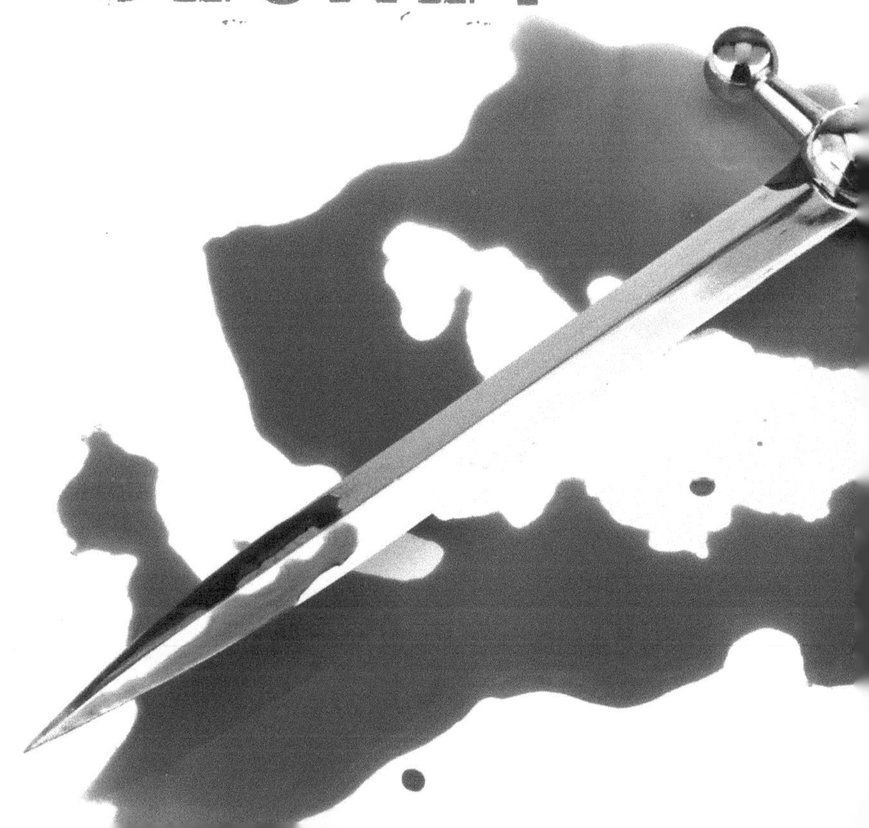

CHAPTER 1

Inside the Mind of a Killer

A QUESTION THAT HAS BAFFLED science for centuries—what exactly makes a killer? Is it all about instability in a person's life, like Jeffrey Dahmer, who started dismembering his victims at a mere eighteen years old? Are killers the result of a single-parented household like Ted Bundy, who was raised by his teenage mother? Or maybe killers just enjoy the merciless killing, like Jack the Ripper, who inevitably killed over a hundred people?

Whatever the reason, or lack thereof, it is obvious that killers have a disconnection in their brains that make them see the world differently—empty, meaningless, and simply something that can be completely destroyed without a second thought.

Maybe Mommy never hugged them and said she loved them, or their alcoholic family abused them in every way possible. Although horrible, this is not a reason to take another person's life; and yet in a killer's mind, this is more than enough of a reason.

Going a little deeper down the rabbit hole, maybe these psychos do what they do just for the thrill of it, or maybe even get some sort of sexual pleasure from overpowering another human being. As for me, I say, just go ride a roller coaster or go skydiving—something that doesn't permanently affect someone else's life in a negative way! Only if it were that easy for some people, the world would be a much better place.

Alas, some people need to know they are inflicting the deepest, most brutal kind of pain imaginable on others to feel anything. It could be anything from a defenseless animal to a baby, any minor child, or even a spouse. Sadly, it is the ones we love the most do that do the most damage. Not always physically but mentally and emotionally as well.

Even crazier, some people like me try to understand this deranged maniac of a being when in reality, there is no answer, no solution, and most of the time, no hope. There are truly good people in this world; they may be cranky at times because they had a bad day or had something unexpected happen in their life, but generally, most people are good. Most, but not all, there are those select few who simply don't want to be good, and their sole purpose is to create havoc and disruption on earth and in a person's life.

Most killers have some sort of motive, whether it be for love, money, jealousy, fame, or just to feel like they have power over something for once in their lives. I'm not going to sit here and preach to you how murder is wrong and you shouldn't do it because, well, that is just obvious. My objective is one that is a little more complex—to try and put some sort of meaning to why people do the things they do.

I know that previously I said there was no understanding, and sometimes there isn't, but if there is even the slightest bit of comfort I can provide someone in understanding such an evil in this world, then it is worth it. If discussing this issue and making people aware of these monsters can help them recognize these actions before tragedy strikes and help them stay clear of that person from the very beginning, then I have done my civic duty.

Most people when they hear the word *killer* just think of the literal meaning of the word and think of the next Charles Manson. Unfortunately, there are many different ways to kill someone. The ways I want to focus on are the mental, emotional, and psychological ways to break down and kill someone.

Of course there will be skeptics out there who will just dismiss these words, saying, "How in the world can you kill someone without even touching them?" Well, this book is going to explore that theory in depth. Even more so, this is not just a book, but the events in the book are closely related to what occurred in my life and how I was able to break free and live again.

Sometimes people are afraid to talk about their bad experiences because they feel like it's stupid, their fault, no one would care, it happens all the time, etc. But I'm here to tell whoever is reading this that it was not your fault what someone else did to you. You do not deserve to be treated that way, and you can and should use your voice to speak up about it and prevent it from happening to others.

CHAPTER 2

Meeting the Monster

A KILLER, OR A SOCIOPATH in general, is not easy to spot. Actually they have trained themselves to be your typical average Joe who couldn't even be picked out of a crowd. So how do you spot this person? Sadly, you don't. They spot you!

A person with some kind of agenda, a killer in this case, often has a "rule book" or some type of guidelines that they follow in order to capture and lure in their prey. Not to sound too much like a lion hunting in the wild, but that is exactly what a killer does—he stalks and hunts his prey.

It was an ordinary day like all the rest—you get up, get dressed, get on the bus, go to work, come home, eat dinner, walk the dog, and go to bed. But today was not like those other days—not in the slightest. Natalie was on the bus, on her way home from the office—tired, beaten down, and just wanting to lounge back in her favorite chair at home and go to sleep. Natalie was nothing special. There was no kind of drama in her life, and she liked it that way.

Natalie was a paralegal and worked in a huge law firm. Her day was spent dealing with lawyers, interviewing clients, and doing her typical contract work. Although mundane sometimes, Natalie absolutely loved her job and wouldn't dream of doing anything else. Working as a paralegal gave her a sense of purpose. She loved being able to help people and be the left hand of justice!

Five o'clock often came around quickly for Natalie, and this day was no different. She shut her computer down, locked all of her files up, and headed out the door. She said goodbye to Ted and Frank

Kuzak (the two lawyers), grabbed her coat, and headed out the big glass doors to go home. As Natalie was walking to her bus stop, she thought about a particular case from that day about a girl whose boyfriend had turned against her for leaving him and who did all kinds of damage to her and her life.

But that was work, and she wanted to leave it at work so she could enjoy her evening. When Natalie got to the bus stop, she saw an old couple waiting there, both with walkers, and they still looked so in love. How Natalie longed for this: to have someone by her side that loved her unconditionally—a man whom she could come home to and start a family of her own with.

Natalie's thoughts were abruptly interrupted by a bus driver shouting at her, "Are you coming or not?"

Natalie got herself together and boarded the bus, sitting at the back like she usually does. The ride home was the same as most days—mothers and their kids screaming, people listening to music, and others sleeping or reading.

When Natalie's bus finally reached her neighborhood, she got off and walked home. On her way home, she was thinking about all of the things she had to do for the night. First was to take Rufus for a walk. Who is Rufus you may be wondering? None other than Natalie's best legged friend. Little did Natalie know this was going to be the start of something much more sinister. As Natalie was walking down the street with Rufus, she noticed a tall figure in the distance. This figure seemed to be walking toward her but suddenly stopped and sat on a bench.

Not thinking much of it, Natalie and Rufus continued their walk down the street, toward the bench where the man was now sitting. Rufus has always been a loving and playful dog, but this day, as he passed the man on the bench, of course he decided to pee on the corner where the man was sitting! Humiliated, Natalie immediately apologized to the man, turning beet red as she scolded Rufus. Although upset, the man gave a smile and said, "No harm done."

Natalie still apologized repeatedly and asked the man if there was anything she could do to apologize. Unexpectedly, the handsome stranger said that he would like to have coffee with her sometime. A bit confused at his request, Natalie accepted the man's offer and wrote her phone number on a napkin for him. As Natalie was handing him the napkin, he said, "Thank you. I will give you a call sometime. By the way, the name's John."

Apologizing once more, Natalie left to continue her walk with Rufus, replaying the peculiar events that just took place. *He probably won't even call,* she thought. *After all, my dog just peed on the man for crying out loud!*

About thirty minutes later, Natalie and Rufus arrived back home. Both tired and sweaty, Natalie crashed on the couch as Rufus headed to his water bowl.

Natalie noticed the red light was blinking on her answering machine, so she hit play. The first message was from her mother, reminding her of a lunch they were having later that week, and the second message was her dentist's office confirming her appointment the next day, but the third message was, "Hey, Natalie, this is John. I hope it's not too soon to call you about coffee, but your dog did pee on me, so I figured this would be a good icebreaker. Call me back so we can set up a day soon. My number is 524-634-7588. Hope to hear from you soon."

If only Natalie ignored that message, she would have saved herself from so much pain.

CHAPTER 3

The Chase

IGNORING JOHN'S MESSAGE, NATALIE went in the kitchen to start making dinner. Every night, it was just her and Rufus, so she made extra food just for him. When Natalie and Rufus had finished eating, Natalie let Rufus out into the backyard as she curled up on the couch. She finally had some me-time, she thought, and turned on the TV.

After about half an hour, she went outside and said, "Rufus, time to come home," and he came barreling in the door. As she walked over to sit back down on the couch, of course, Rufus felt obliged to join her. Natalie grabbed Rufus and hugged him tight, telling him how much she loved him.

As soon as she let go, Rufus jumped down and went to his bed. Natalie continued to flip through the channels, but there was nothing on. She decided to pop in a movie and just unwind for a bit longer. *But what to watch*, she wondered, and then, in the corner, she saw *Love Actually*. *This is a weird coincidence*, she thought, but she loved that movie, so she put it in.

Once her movie was done, it was time for a shower and then bed. She started to head down the long hall toward the shower when she started thinking about John's message. *Maybe I'll give him a call really quick. There's no harm in that, right?*

Natalie picked up the phone and started dialing John's number. She was admittedly nervous because of what happened earlier, and she did think he was really cute! After three rings, John answered, "Hello?"

"Hi, John, this is Natalie from earlier tonight."

"Oh, I was wondering when I would be hearing from you. How are you, my dear?"

"Good, John. I mean still embarrassed about what Rufus did to you, but I'm actually calling to set up our date."

"Oh, it's a date now?"

"Oh no! I mean our coffee."

"Ha ha, relax. I'm glad you said date. How does tomorrow night around seven work?"

"That sounds great, John! There is a nice little coffee shop around the corner!"

"Yes, I know that place very well, Lucky Leaf. My friend is the manager over there. So I will see you tomorrow at seven there!"

"Great, John! See you then. Bye!"

Feeling all giddy about her date, Natalie continued to the bathroom to take her shower. As she was showering, she couldn't help but hum and sing as she was so happy! She made up little songs like "I have a date tomorrow, tomorrow, tomorrow with this guy I know! John will meet me tomorrow, tomorrow, tomorrow at seven!" Natalie definitely wasn't holding her breath for a Grammy on that one, but she was just so happy how things were playing out.

Once done and ready for bed, she wrote a special note in her phone reminding her of her date with John with kissy faces and hearts. She couldn't stop smiling and thinking about him. She even thought of all the different things they could do together, all the places they could go!

She thought that maybe this could be fate! Maybe she was finally going to be like that old couple she saw standing at the bus stop! She thought maybe this was destiny and was always supposed to happen this way, and it all started in the funniest way with her best friend!

Natalie calmed herself down as much as she could and called her mom to tell her the good news. When Natalie's mom, Rebecca, answered the phone, she sounded groggy.

"Mom, it's me! Did I wake you up?"

"Yes, Natalie, but I'm always glad to hear from my favorite daughter."

"Mom, I'm your only daughter."

"But still, you're the best one! Now what's wrong, my girl?"

"For the first time, nothing is wrong. Quite the opposite, things are perfect!"

"Oh really, and why is that baby?"

"Well, Mom, I met a guy, and he wants to take me out tomorrow! Funny story, Rufus actually peed on him, and that is how we met, but for some reason, he asked me out afterward!"

"Wait, wait, wait, Rufus peed on him, and he still asked you out? I'm so happy for you, baby, but I can't believe that was his reaction! He must be some kind of guy!"

"I know, Mom. I am so excited for tomorrow, I can barely contain myself. But I do have to go to bed so I can catch the 6:00 a.m. bus tomorrow. I just wanted to tell you my great news! Good night, Mom!"

"Good night, baby! Just be careful, and take care of yourself!"

CHAPTER 4

Cat and Mouse

AT WORK THE NEXT day, Natalie kept daydreaming about her upcoming date with John. As she was imagining what she was going to wear, Mr. Kuzak said, "Are you done with those briefs yet, Natalie?"

Natalie quickly snapped back to reality and gave an abrupt, "Almost finished, Mr. Kuzak. I'm putting the finishing touches on the last page."

Mr. Kuzak shook his head and walked away.

Natalie realized that she couldn't be doing that at work, but she was just so excited for her first date in over a year! She finished up her brief and took it to Mr. Kuzak's office, apologizing again for not having finished it before. He smiled at her, nodded his head, and asked her to close the door on her way out.

Because Natalie had been working at the firm for almost five years, Mr. Kuzak gave her a little more leeway than he would with most of his paralegals. Natalie went back to her desk and began researching a new upcoming client but quickly found herself thinking about John again.

"Why am I making such a big deal out of this? It's just coffee!"

At that very moment, her cell phone vibrated. It was a text from, guess who, John! It was a cute picture of him with the words, "Looking forward to tonight!" This just added to Natalie's excitement and made the rest of the day drag on for what seemed like forever.

Natalie tried her hardest to keep herself busy with routine paperwork and continued research. By lunchtime, she had actually gotten over halfway through her workload for the day. On her lunch break in the cafeteria, she figured she would give John a call—no answer, which disappointed her, but she received a text right after from him. "Sorry, I can't answer right now. In the middle of a meeting. Can't wait to see you!"

This brought the biggest smile to Natalie's face! She was so nervous, she didn't eat but had a soda, hoping it would give her energy to finish her day. When she got back to her desk, she started filing pending cases in her desk drawer and locking them away. The rest of the day was slow—just copying and faxing documents and getting the lawyers' signatures on a few things.

It was finally time to go home. Natalie hurried out of the office with only brief "Good nights" to Ted and Frank. As she anxiously waited for her bus, she looked at her phone for the first time since lunch. It was a message from John that read, "I'm so sorry, Natalie, but I have to take my car to the shop tonight and can't make our date. Rain check?" At first, Natalie was angry and annoyed. She didn't know what to think. John had been texting her all day, letting her know he was going to see her tonight and how happy he was. How could things change so quickly?

After boarding the bus, Natalie sat down and thought about the whole situation and how much she wanted to see John tonight. She took her phone out of her purse and dialed his number.

"Hello?"

"Hi, John, this is Natalie."

"Natalie, hey! I'm so sorry about tonight. Please forgive me!"

"It's okay, John. At first, I was upset, and then I realized these kinds of things happen all the time. How about I come pick you up for our date tonight?"

"You would do that? Absolutely! Same time?"

"Same time. I'll see you at seven, John. Can't wait!"

"Thank you so much, sweetie! See you at seven!"

After hanging up, Natalie felt the butterflies come back, and everything in her world was okay again. She didn't even realize she was on the phone so long, her stop was next. As she pulled the rope, letting the bus driver know to stop, she gathered her things and got off the bus, waving to the bus driver. On her walk home, she kept smiling thinking about John. As she turned the key to her house, Rufus greeted her with a sloppy kiss and a bark.

"Time to go outside, boy!" She took him out to sniff around and pee and then took him back inside and gave him a can of dog chow. "Sorry, boy, but Mommy can't eat with you tonight. I have a date!"

After Natalie put the dog bowl on the ground, she went into her bedroom to change. She took a look through her clothes and pulled out a pink summer dress. *This is perfect!* she thought. She quickly changed and headed to the car, patting Rufus on the head as she left.

Once in the car, she called John to find out where to pick him up. The phone rang twice, and she heard, "Natalie?"

"Hi, John. I'm ready to pick you up. I just need an address."

"Sure, and thank you so much again, sweetheart! My address is 561 Stalkhome Street, Quinoia 15987."

"Great! I'll see you soon, John!"

As Natalie left her driveway, she had a weird feeling. It wasn't a scary or happy feeling, but she couldn't quite put her finger on it. She ignored it and continued to Stalkhome Street.

Upon arriving, John hopped in her car, holding a single red rose. He said, "This is for you." She blushed, said thank you, and headed to the Lucky Leaf.

Once there, Natalie parked the car and turned off the engine. John quickly turned to her and said, "Wait here for a second."

She was confused but did as he requested. He jumped out of the car, ran around it, and opened her door. Natalie wasn't often taken for surprise but, *A rose and opening the car door for me on the first date? Things are going better than I expected.*

Natalie thanked John and stepped out of the car. As she turned around to walk toward the entrance, she noticed that John had grabbed her hand with a soft embrace and smiled at her. *This was perfect!* she thought.

As they got to the entrance of the Lucky Leaf, John again held the door open for Natalie. She thanked him and walked hand in hand up to the cash register.

"What are you kids having tonight?" the lady behind the cash register asked.

"Just two small coffees," Natalie replied.

"Are you sure, hun? It's on me!"

Natalie blushed again and shook her head yes.

The cashier said, "That'll be $3.50."

John handed her the money, took the coffees, and sat down with Natalie. Natalie was simply starstruck by John—his behavior, the way he carried himself—she was so happy! As they talked and sipped coffee, Natalie grew more and more fond of John. They seemed to have so many things in common and wanted the same things in life.

When finished with their coffees, John threw the cups away and left for the car with Natalie. He held every door for her, just as he did before, and they laughed the whole way home. When Natalie got to John's driveway, he leaned over and gave her a light kiss on the lips.

"I hope that was okay," John said. "Tonight just went so well, and you are such a beautiful woman. Any man would be crazy not to be attracted to such a beauty!"

"I feel the same way, John. I'm glad you did! Can we do this again?"

"Absolutely! You have a good night, dear. I know I will with you in my dreams."

John smiled and shut the car door, and Natalie pulled away. She still couldn't believe the night that she had. It was like a dream that she never wanted to wake up from! As she pulled into her driveway and got out of the car, she thought she saw a red light under her car but couldn't see anything now. She brushed it off and turned the key to her apartment door. There was Rufus, her best friend, happy as always to greet her.

As she took him outside to go to the bathroom, she couldn't stop thinking about John. Once Rufus did his thing, they went back inside, and Natalie got ready for bed. She climbed into bed, pulled the covers up over her head, and drifted off as she thought how perfect her life was right now.

CHAPTER 5

Gotcha!

WAKING UP THE NEXT morning, Natalie felt like a brand-new woman! She was happy, excited for the day, and full of energy! As she was getting ready for work, she was singing and dancing. Rufus was even confused by this behavior. As she went to let him outside, she gave him a big kiss and said, "Who's the best dog ever? YOU!"

Natalie twirled into the kitchen, laughing and humming, and poured herself a cup of coffee. She felt like this was the start of her new life, her future. She finished getting dressed for work, let Rufus inside, and ran out the house to catch her bus. As always, the bus driver smiled at her and said good morning, but this morning, Natalie replied, "And what a glorious morning it is!" Natalie took her seat on the bus with the other passengers, and the bus took off.

Everyone around Natalie could notice there was something different about her—a glow that almost radiated to anyone around her. Surprisingly, Natalie's phone started to ring. *Who could this possibly be, this early in the morning?* she wondered. It was none other than her beloved John! Natalie quickly answered, "Hello?"

"Natalie! Good morning. It's John. I couldn't stop thinking about last night and how much fun it was!"

"Yes, it was a lot of fun! I hope we can do something again soon!"

"Oh, I'm so glad you said that, Natalie, because I was thinking we could go to a movie or something tonight?"

"Oh, that sounds great, John! Should I meet you at the theater?"

"Actually, why don't we just ride together? You don't mind picking me up at my house, do you?"

"Of course not! Seven again?"

"That's perfect! Thank you so much, Natalie. I'm so excited to see you!"

"Me, too, John. I'm almost at work, but I'll call you later."

"Great, hun. See you later! Have a great day!"

"You, too, John. Bye."

As Natalie hung up the phone, she couldn't help but think it was a little strange how he wanted her to pick him up again, but she was so excited that she had actually found a great guy that she didn't give it too much thought.

After Natalie got off the bus and walked into work, everyone could sense there was something different about her. Not bad, just different, which caused a lot of suspicion around the office. Fred approached Natalie's desk and greeted her good morning. He told her that they were having a deposition at 11:00 a.m., and he needed her there to help take notes. Natalie smiled and said, "My pleasure, Fred. Anything else I can do for you?"

Fred was a bit startled by the eagerness in her voice but ignored it and said, "That will be all, Natalie, besides your normal work."

She smiled and nodded as she unlocked files in her desk to work on.

When Fred walked away, Natalie checked her phone and found a text from John.

"Miss you, hun!"

Natalie smiled and got the butterflies in her stomach. Instead of doing her work, she ended up texting back and forth with John until 11:00 a.m., when Frank came up to her desk and told her to go to the upstairs conference room with her paper and pen. The deposition was very long and boring and took three hours to complete. Afterward, Natalie was exhausted. Luckily, as soon as the client left, Frank announced, "Okay, it's finally lunchtime, guys! Meet me back in the conference room in an hour, and we can go over how to handle this case going forward."

Natalie pushed her chair back and rushed out of the conference room and back to her desk to grab her phone. There was another text from John. It just said, "Go down to the cafeteria." This was odd, but she was starving so didn't question it. As Natalie boarded the elevator to go downstairs, she was all smiles, thinking about tonight. As the elevator got to the ground level and opened, she was greeted by John. She was shocked and had no clue what to think. She was happy but immediately said, "John, what are you doing at my work?"

"I came to surprise you. I thought you would be happy, but your reaction tells me otherwise."

"No, no. Of course, I'm happy to see you. I'm sorry. Let me grab a sandwich, and we can talk."

Natalie, still in shock, went through the line at the cafeteria and grabbed a ham sandwich and an iced tea. After she paid, she looked around and went to go sit with John. That walk across the cafeteria felt like the longest walk of her life. She had so many thoughts whirling through her mind. She got to the table and sat across from John.

"I thought we were meeting tonight?"

"We are, babe. I just wanted to surprise you and make your day a little brighter."

At the moment, he handed her a single red rose. She was smiling like a Cheshire cat and apologized to him again for seeming upset or ungrateful.

"No, hun, it's perfectly fine."

"I do have to ask. How did you know where I worked?"

"You told me last night, silly!"

Natalie thought about this for a moment, and she most certainly never told him where she worked. Natalie was a very private person and avoided questions pertaining to her personal life. But she liked John so much, she didn't want to risk making him angry by saying no, she didn't. So she accepted that maybe she did tell him and forgot. She was tired last night from a long day at work.

"Oh, you're right. I'm sorry, John."

Time seemed to fly by as she finished her lunch, and they talked and laughed and planned their night together. Natalie looked down at her watch, and it was 3:00 p.m. already! "Oh no, I'm so late!"

Natalie apologized as she ran to the elevator. As she boarded the elevator, all she could think about was how mad her bosses were going to be. When she arrived at her floor, she sped to the conference room, but it was empty.

Her head immediately fell into her hands, and she took a deep breath, dreading what was awaiting her. She knew she had to go to her boss's office and try to explain, but she had no idea where to even start. She screwed up. This whole day was turning into a complete mess, and she was beyond overwhelmed with it all.

Arriving at Frank's office, she gently knocked.

"Come in," a gruff voice replied.

"Hi, sir. I'm so sorry I missed the meeting."

"Close the door, Natalie. I think we need to talk."

"Natalie, what is going on? The last few days, you have been completely distracted, not getting your work done, and the work you have done is late and lacking."

"Sir, I'm so sorry. It won't happen again!"

"Natalie, you have been with this office for some time, and I like you. I really do. But I can't ignore not getting your work done, doing a sloppy job, and missing important meetings. I think you need to take some time off and collect yourself."

"No, sir, I'm fine. I swear!"

"Natalie, I wasn't asking. Get your things at your desk and go home. I will call you when you can come back. I'm sorry, Natalie, but this is the best thing for the office and for you."

Natalie was crushed. This job was her life! But what was she to do? She had no choice but to do as Frank said. So she turned around, left his office, and slowly closed the door. As Natalie gathered her things at her desk, her enthusiastic behavior was no more. There was no glow, no laughter, but there was a single tear that slowly ran down her cheek as she exited the building.

When she got to the bus stop, she sat on the bench and called John. At this point, she was completely sobbing and slightly hyperventilating.

"Hello?"

"Natalie? Hi, hun! Aren't you at work?"

"I got fired, John!"

"Oh no, hun! Why? It wasn't because of me, was it?"

"No, John, I was the one who screwed up and slacked off. I have no clue what I'm going to do now!"

"Relax, sweetheart. We will figure it out. Just focus on tonight for now."

"Thanks, John. That actually really helps. I should go and get myself together. I will see you in a few hours. Bye."

"It will all be okay. Don't worry, hun! Bye for now!"

CHAPTER 6

Too Good to Be True

STEPPING OFF THE BUS for the last time, Natalie was hit with a sudden rush of emotion and burst into tears. That final walk home was the longest and most depressing walk of her life. She kept replaying Frank's last words in her head, "Get your things at your desk and go home." It was still like a knife to the gut.

Despite everything, Natalie was still enthusiastic about life. I mean, she did just meet a great guy, right? Natalie wiped the tears away as she unlocked her front door. Naturally, Rufus was right there to greet her with a big sloppy kiss! She closed the front door and let Rufus out in the backyard while she was getting ready for her date.

Natalie went straight to the bathroom and hopped into the shower, hoping to wash this terrible day away. When she was done and all dried off, she went to her bedroom and picked out her favorite red dress to wear. She couldn't explain it, but somehow, the thought of seeing John tonight made all of her problems disappear.

Natalie laid her dress on the bed, went out of her bedroom, closed the bedroom door, and opened the door leading to the backyard. He was already waiting at the door for her with that goofy grin only he gives her. She laughed as she opened the door. "Come on in here, ya goofball, and Mommy will get you some dinner."

Rufus ran inside the house and sat right in the middle of the kitchen floor, just waiting for his dinner. Natalie made his favorite—kibble with gravy and chicken!

As Rufus slurped up his dinner, Natalie went to do her hair and makeup. She dried and straightened her hair and applied the most beautiful sparkly pink blush and eye shadow. Dressing up made Natalie feel a lot better about herself—hopeful about the future. Now it was time to put on the perfect dress and heels for the perfect guy! She felt like a million bucks! Well, almost.

Walking out the door, Natalie told Rufus she would be back soon and pet his head. As she was heading to her car, she called John to tell him she was on her way. The phone rang about three times before John answered, "Hello, beautiful!"

"Hi, John. I'm on my way. Are you ready?"

"Yes, dear."

"Perfect. I'll see you soon! Bye."

As Natalie pulled out of her driveway, she felt a little bit uneasy; she didn't know why, but she just brushed it off as being nervous. When she arrived at John's place, he waved to her and got in the car. As soon as he got in, he told her he knew how upset she must be, but tonight was going to be the start of a brand-new chapter, and he gave her a hug!

This helped her feel so much better. She thanked him and continued their trip to the movies. When they arrived at the theater, there didn't seem to be any place to park. John told Natalie she could pull up to the door and go inside and he would park the car for her. She happily obliged because she had a long and stressful day. Natalie put the car in park and started to unbuckle her seatbelt, and by that time, John was able to open the door for her. She loved this royal treatment and was quickly falling for John.

Natalie gave John her hand as she got out of the car, and she thanked him as she went into the theater. Once in the theater, she looked at the list of movies playing at that time. She wasn't sure what John wanted to go see, but there was one movie playing that she had been wanting to see for a while—*Ready or Not*! It was a drama/thriller about a couple who had just gotten married, and now the new bride was fighting for her life from his deranged family! A few minutes later, John walked into the theater, and Natalie told him she really wanted to see *Ready or Not*, but it was up to him. He immediately said, "No way!" and Natalie was disappointed, but said, "Okay, then, what do you want to see?"

He said, "No, hun. I meant, no way, I was going to pick that same movie!"

Natalie was so happy, and they got in line.

When they got up to the cashier, John handed the lady his credit card and said, "Two to *Ready or Not*."

The lady smiled, rang his card up, and handed him the tickets. Natalie and John walked up to the usher and handed him the tickets.

"Natalie?" John said. "This is embarrassing, but would you mind buying the drinks and popcorn? I'm a bit short on money this week."

Natalie was a little surprised, but she was so happy to be on a date with him that she happily bought the drinks and popcorn.

Much to her surprise, John handed Natalie her ticket while he went inside the theater. She was more than a little upset that he left her to buy the snacks and didn't even stand in line with her to help carry everything to the theater. Once everything was purchased, she headed to the theatre, and of course, everything was dark by the time she arrived.

She quietly whispered for John, and instead of coming over to help her, he waved at her to come over to where he was sitting. As she got to the seat, John said, "Thank you so much for getting this, and I'm sorry I didn't stand with you. I just wanted to make sure we got good seats. It was the least I could do for you after your day."

Although still a little upset, this made sense to her, and she got comfortable in her seat.

Once the movie started, Natalie noticed something unusual. John was holding her hand! She was happily surprised, smiled, and continued to watch the movie. Every time there was a scary scene and Natalie jumped, John would put his arm around her and rub her shoulder. By the end of the movie, Natalie felt like she had known John forever and was very comfortable being around him.

Walking out of the theater hand in hand with John, Natalie felt like she was floating on cloud nine. She thought, *Maybe this is what they mean by "When one door closes, another one opens"?* She was so caught up in her thoughts, she didn't even hear John ask her what she thought about the movie.

"What?" Natalie replied.

John laughed and asked again, "What did you think about the movie?"

"I really liked it!"

"Good, me too!"

They walked through the sea of people to get to the car. The whole way home, they were talking about the movie and all of the people that went to see it that night. As they pulled into John's driveway, he turned to her and told him what a great time he had. She said that she did too and was so glad that she got to see him tonight. As he started to open the door to get out, he turned back to her and asked her if it was okay if he gave her a good night kiss. She blushed and said okay. John leaned in and gave her a soft kiss on the lips. He smiled and got out of the car with a seductive "Good night."

Natalie felt like she was a little school girl with a crush! She was so happy that losing her job wasn't even on her mind. All the way home, she couldn't stop smiling and thinking about John—how he made her feel when they were together and even when they weren't together. Upon pulling into her driveway, her phone went off with a text. DING, DING. It was John! The message read, "I had such a wonderful night with you, Natalie. You looked simply stunning in your red dress. I'm sorry I didn't say anything. You just took my breath away! I know this is crazy because we haven't known each other long, but I am starting to develop a real feeling for you!"

Natalie couldn't believe what she was reading. Could he actually be THE ONE! She was so ecstatic reading this and had to tell someone right now. She ran inside, greeted Rufus, let him outside, and called her mom.

"MOM, YOU AREN'T GOING TO BELIEVE THIS!"

"What's wrong, dear? Are you okay?"

"I'm better than okay, Mom. I'm great! I think I could have met the perfect guy for me!"

"Slow down, dear. Tell me everything."

"Well, his name is John. We have gone out a few times now, and I really like him. He treats me like a princess, and when I'm with him, it feels like everything is okay with the world. I lost my job today, and he made me forget all about it."

"WHAT! You lost your job? I'm so sorry, dear. What happened?"

"I really don't want to talk about it, Mom. It will just make me upset again."

"I understand, sweetheart, but what are you going to do about your bills? About Rufus?"

"Mom, this is why I didn't want to tell you. You always do this, and I just want to be happy right now. So PLEASE!"

"Okay, sweetheart. I understand, and I'm sorry. I just worry about you. Well, I'm always here if you need me. Just take things slow with this boy. You don't need to be rushing into anything right now."

"Okay, Mom. I love you, but I have to go."

"Okay, dear. Take care. Good night."

Natalie hung up the phone and rolled her eyes as she fell backward onto the couch. *Mothers*, she thought and went to let Rufus in so somebody could be happy for her.

Rufus ran through the door and jumped right on the couch. As Natalie closed the back door, there was a knock on her front door. It was 11:00 p.m. *Who could it possibly be at this hour?* she thought. It was John! She lit up immediately and smiled.

"I just dropped you off silly. What are you doing here?"

"I wanted to make sure you made it home okay, and I figured since it was Friday night, I would come over, and we could watch some TV on the couch."

She stepped back and motioned him to come in.

"RUFUS! Hey, buddy, how are you doing?"

Much to Natalie's surprise, Rufus was very happy to see John and laid on his lap as soon as he sat on the couch. Natalie smiled, walked over to the couch, and sat beside John. As she turned the TV guide on, she asked him what he wanted to watch.

"Surprise me!" he said, putting his arm around her.

As she flipped through the TV guide, she found *Must Love Dogs* and pushed play.

"Oh, I love this movie!" she said as they snuggled up closer.

About halfway through the movie, Natalie caught herself falling asleep. She told John she really appreciated his coming over, but she was just so tired. She asked him if maybe they could do something tomorrow when he got off work. He smiled and said he would be happy to.

He stood up and started to walk to the door, still holding hands with Natalie. As she opened the door and thanked him again, he leaned in and gave her another kiss—this time, pulling her into him for a few seconds.

"Good night, baby, miss you already!"

"Good night, hun. I'll see you tomorrow."

CHAPTER 7

Drama, Drama, Drama

WAKING UP THE NEXT morning was very surreal for Natalie—getting up knowing she no longer had a job or any idea what to do next. As she got out of bed and started her day, she moved through her morning routine almost zombie-like. She let Rufus out to the bathroom and started to make her coffee, but she felt this overwhelming sensation come over her—not sadness but freedom.

For the first time in over four years, Natalie had nowhere she needed to be—no files to sort nor research to do. She could sit on the couch with Rufus and her coffee and actually watch the morning news! After Natalie had started the coffee, she grabbed Rufus's food bowl to give him breakfast. She only had one can of Alpo left, so she would have to go to the store later. Now her feeling of freedom quickly turned to fear.

What will she do for money? How is she going to pay her rent, bills, food, and take care of Rufus? Natalie was freaking out! And what do we all do when we freak out but call our mom!

"Hello?"

"Mom, I don't have a job, and I need to go to the store! I'm going to go broke! I'm going to have to give up my apartment and live on the streets! I'm going to have to beg for food! Mom, HELP!"

"Slow down, slow down, Natalie! I knew it would take a little time for this to sink in, but I am glad you are starting to think about these things. Now let's approach this rationally. You have a savings, right?"

"Yes, but it's not a whole lot."

"But at least it's something, dear, to get you by for a few days."

"Ya, you're right."

"Good. Now have you updated your résumé?"

"No, not yet."

"Well, you need to do that, dear, and then start applying for jobs like you did before. Baby girl, you've got this! I know you're scared, but you have been here before and look how far you have come! And I will always be there for you if you need me."

"Thank you, Mom! You always know how to make me feel so much better! I have to go let Rufus in, but then I will start getting ready for my new life!"

"That's my girl! Call me later if you need to. Love you. Bye, baby!"

"Bye, Mom."

After speaking with her mom, Natalie felt so much better. She could actually breathe again! With a deep exhale, she opened the back door to let Rufus in. "Come on, buddy, breakfast time!"

Instead of watching TV, Natalie poured herself a cup of coffee and went over to the computer.

"Okay, time to make a change!" she said to herself. As the computer loaded, she sipped on her coffee and noticed that music was playing. It was her phone. She put her coffee down and walked to the bedroom to get it.

"Hello?"

"Hey, babe, just calling to check on you. How are you feeling?"

"Hi, John. I'm okay. I had a nice talk with my mother, and right now, I am updating my résumé and applying for jobs."

"Good for you. I'm so proud of you! You will be on your feet again in no time! Hey, I have to go. Dinner tonight?"

"That sounds great, hun! Pick you up at seven?"

"Yes please, hun! Gotta run, bye!"

It slightly bothered her how she always had to pick him up, but overall, it wasn't that big a deal. She left the phone in her bedroom and walked back out to the computer. It was 8:00 a.m., and she figured she had plenty of time.

Natalie opened up the word file that contained her résumé and started to add her past job and all of her duties. She did so many things at the law firm, it was actually difficult to write them all down. As a paralegal, she did everything a typical paralegal does and typical office work that a secretary or executive assistant would do.

When Natalie finished up on her résumé and she felt that it was perfect, she saved the file and closed it. By this time, she was starting to get hungry. "It's eleven. No wonder I'm hungry! And, Rufus, I bet you have to go outside again."

Getting up from her desk, she stretched and yawned and went to let Rufus out. He danced around in circles until Natalie opened the door releasing him. Then she went into the kitchen and opened the refrigerator, trying to decide what to eat.

"Hmmm, I don't really feel like cooking something. Maybe I'll just make a quick peanut butter and jelly sandwich." With this, she closed the refrigerator and got everything out to make her sandwich. Once her sandwich was made, she let Rufus in and sat on the couch. Of course, Rufus had to sit with her, and he happily shared her sandwich with her also!

"Okay, that's enough of a break. Time to get back to work!" She walked over to the computer, opened up the Internet, and proceeded to search for a few job boards. Rufus, on the other hand, continued to stretch out across the couch and take a nap. Natalie looked over at him and smiled and returned to her current task. "Hmmm, not a lot of paralegal jobs available near me." This was a surprise. She had thought a paralegal would be in high demand. And they used to be, just not anymore.

With the changing times, Natalie was discovering it wasn't going to be easy to get another paralegal job. *Better broaden my horizons,* she thought. Administrative assistant—she had kind of done that in her previous work, so she applied to this job and jobs like it. After several more hours of applying to jobs, her eyes started to hurt. "Okay, Rufus, I think I'm calling it a day for this!" Rufus was still sleeping and couldn't care less.

As she shut off the computer, she stood up to walk into her room. Two missed calls and five texts—all from John. Natalie called him back, and he gruffly answered, "Hello."

"John, hi. I'm sorry I missed your calls and texts. I've been busy."

"Why didn't you have you phone with you? You're not at work. I was worried."

This hurt Natalie's feelings but didn't want to let him know, and she just said, "I know. I'm sorry. Are we still getting dinner tonight?"

"I don't know, Natalie. I'm pretty upset."

Not worrying about not having a job but just trying to save her relationship, she said, "How about I buy dinner to make it up to you?"

There was a pause for a few moments followed by, "I guess that's okay. I'll see you at seven. Bye."

"I'm sorry again, hun. Bye."

Natalie had no idea what she was getting herself into, but honestly, she would never have listened to reason at this point anyway. She was under John's spell and just wanted him to stay with her.

Natalie brushed the phone call off and headed to the bathroom to take a shower and get ready for dinner. She loved getting ready for dates; it made her feel special and actually wanted by someone. She hadn't felt this way for a while, and it was long overdue.

Getting out of the shower, she wrapped a towel around herself and went into her bedroom with Rufus following her. He started to lick the water off of her legs, and she yelled, "RUFUS, NOW YOU STOP THAT!" He looked startled but just turned around and left the room.

As Natalie was picking out her outfit, John called, "Hey, babe, would you mind picking me up now instead of seven?"

"I haven't done my hair yet."

"Oh, hun, you're always beautiful to me! Please?"

Natalie blushed. "Of course, hun."

Natalie put on her shoes and rushed out the door, petting Rufus goodbye. When she arrived at John's, he was standing in the driveway with his hands behind his back. As Natalie packed the car, John opened the door and told her to close her eyes. She was a little put off and nervous about his request, but she closed her eyes anyway.

John said, "Okay, you can open your eyes now." It was a picture of them on their first date together outlined in a heart! Natalie was speechless and leaned over to kiss him.

"Thank you so much, hun! This is so sweet and so thoughtful!"

"You're welcome, sweetheart. I just felt really bad about how I reacted earlier. I just had a bad day at work and didn't even think about what you are going through. I also have another big surprise for you once we get to the restaurant!"

Natalie's face beamed! As they were driving to the restaurant, John reached over and put his hand on her leg as she was driving. She looked down and smiled at him. Everything was so perfect! She didn't even think about losing her job. John was going to make sure she was okay.

Once at the restaurant, John opened her door, and they walked hand in hand together. The waiter seated them at a table for two in the back.

"So what is this big surprise?"

"Well, I was going to wait until the end of dinner, but since you are so impatient, I will tell you now."

She laughed and said, "But isn't that why you like me so much?"

He laughed and said, "Since things between us are going so well, I have been talking to my family about you, and they want to meet you. Not only that, but they want to do something special to meet you since I haven't been this happy for a very long time. They actually wanted me to ask you if you will join us on our annual vacation next week!"

"Really? Oh my gosh, this is so exciting! But I don't know, John. There is Rufus and the fact that I just lost my job."

"Babe, babe, relax. I know all of this, but I think a vacation is just what you need right now to clear your head and reenergize."

"You know what? I think you are right! I will make arrangements for my mom to watch Rufus, and we will go on our first vacation together!"

"Great, baby! We are going a few hours away to the beach. Just some fun in the sun to take all of your cares away!"

They were both so enthralled in conversation, they didn't even notice the waiter standing by the table.

"May I take your order?"

"Oh, yes, I'm so sorry. We will both have the pasta and a diet coke. Is that okay for you, dear?" John asked.

A little surprised, but she said, "Yes, that's fine. Thank you."

As the night went on, it seemed to fly by with the talk of upcoming vacation plans. They talked about what they were going to do on vacation and laying out on the beach together. John told Natalie that he had never been to the beach before, and he was very nervous. This only made her feel much more excited and closer to him.

As soon as they both finished their meals, the waiter returned with the check and laid it on the table. Natalie didn't want to make the situation uncomfortable, and since she did say she would get dinner, she reached for the check.

"Are you sure?" John asked.

"Of course," Natalie replied. "I told you I would."

After the bill was paid and the waiter had thanked them both, they stood up to leave. All smiles, the two lovebirds headed out to the car. On the way home, John turned the radio on low to some romance songs. Natalie was in a state of complete bliss. She felt like the happiest woman in the whole world! At that moment though, John's voice snapped her back to reality.

"This is embarrassing, but there is one more thing I forgot to tell you about vacation."

"What is that, hun?"

"Since so many people are coming, we have to take your car. Mine is just so bad on gas."

"That's no problem at all, hun. Why is that embarrassing?"

"Well, there's more. Would you be able to pay for your half? I hate to ask because you just lost your job, but my family can't pay for you and me as well."

"Umm, I'll have to check, but I'm sure I can pull everything together."

"Thanks, babe!

"Thank you! We are going to have some much needed TLC."

CHAPTER 8

A Summer Romance

THE DAY HAD FINALLY come—vacation morning! Right on cue, Rufus greeted Natalie at 8:00 a.m. with a big wet kiss all over her face. "Okay, buddy, okay. Are you ready to go outside?" Even before Natalie had finished her sentence, Rufus had run out of the bedroom and was waiting patiently at the back door. As Natalie stretched and put her slippers on, she also had a certain cheerfulness and spring to her step about her. This was going to be the first ever vacation with John! The first of many she hoped!

Natalie got to the back door and let a very anxious Rufus outside. As she closed the door, she walked into the kitchen to make her coffee and his breakfast, like any other morning. She couldn't help but feel a bit sad because she wouldn't see her beloved Rufus for a whole week, but she knew he was in great hands with her mom.

As she was walking to the back door to let Rufus in, there was a knock on her front door. *Who could this be?* she wondered. It was none other than John, with a great big smile on his face, with his suitcases.

"Good morning, honey! And good morning to you too, Rufus! Are you excited for vacation, baby?"

Slightly startled, Natalie still sweetly replied, "Most definitely, baby! I can't wait to spend our very first vacation together!"

"And this is just the beginning!" John said. "I want us to start taking a vacation every year, sort of like a family getaway together!"

At this, Natalie turned starry-eyed and blushed. "That would be incredible, babe!"

Suddenly, Natalie realized that Rufus's breakfast was still sitting on the counter. She then set it on the floor for him, saying, "What a good boy you were to wait."

While Rufus was eating, John and Natalie packed the car to drive to the beach. The car was loaded so much that you could just barely see out of the back window. And now it was time to get Rufus in the car, but where? Oh yes, Rufus got to ride in the passenger seat while John was stuck in the backseat, not even being able to sit on the seat because of the cooler and all of the stuff.

Of course, the whole way to Rebecca's, John was complaining, but once they finally arrived and dropped Rufus off, everything was all right again. John stayed in the car while Natalie took Rufus inside. Once inside, Natalie hugged and kissed Rufus like she was going off to war for the next year, and finally, her mom told her to wipe those tears away because she was going to have a wonderful time at the beach.

Still suspicious of John, Rebecca told her daughter to have a great time but to remember to be careful and call her as soon as they got there to let her know she was okay.

"Mom, everything is going to be amazing! John takes such good care of me!"

"I know, baby. Just take care of yourself, and please call me!"

"Okay, Mom. I love you, and thank you for watching Rufus!"

"You're welcome, baby. I love you to the moon and back!"

And now their great adventure can finally begin! Seven days and six nights in paradise together, or was it? *Eight hours in the car together, this should be interesting,* Natalie thought. About an hour in, it started—the whining and complaining about how bored John was and how close they were to being there. Thankfully, Natalie had a lot of patience; after all, you don't get to be a successful paralegal without having enough patience to deal with unruly clients and lawyers.

"We are almost there, babe. You knew this was going to be a long day when we started."

"I know, I know. I just didn't realize how uncomfortable it would be sitting in a car for this long."

"Since I'm driving, why don't you put on your headphones, listen to music, and take a nap. By the time you wake up, we should be there."

"Okay, you're right, babe. Thanks."

It wasn't even ten minutes after putting the headphones on that John was asleep.

Thank goodness! Natalie thought. *Now I can concentrate on the road and hopefully get there by the time Mr. Cranky Pants wakes up!*" Natalie turned the car radio on low and started to relax to some soft rock. About thirty minutes later, she saw a sign that read Jersey Shore, Next Exit. This is it! They were here! Natalie could barely contain her excitement and let out a little scream.

John woke up immediately. "What is it, babe? Are you all right?"

"We're here. We're finally here!"

Out the window, they passed bridges, clear blue waters, and sandy beaches. Natalie and John were both all smiles as they got closer to their destination. "The Blue Lagoon, there it is babe! Our hotel for the next week!" As they parked the car in the parking lot, John leaned over and gave Natalie a hug and kiss.

"Thank you for everything, babe! I know I can be a handful sometimes."

Natalie rolled her eyes but replied, "Aw, you're welcome, babe! It was all worth it in the end."

They walked hand in hand into the hotel together, all excited to get their room key and start their very first vacation together!

"Hello, how may I help you?" the desk manager asked.

"Hello, we are here to check in. The room is under Natalie."

"Wonderful! Let's take a look here. Yes, two rooms for seven days and six nights and two beach passes. That will be $1,500 plus an additional $200 refundable room fee. And how would you like to pay?"

Natalie turned to John. "That's only $850 apiece, not too bad. How are you paying for yours?"

"Umm, hun, I was hoping you would be willing to help me out on my half. Not all, just $200."

"John! This is something you should have told me before and not right now at the desk! I'll cover you, but this is so not okay!"

"I know, I know. I'm sorry, babe, but thank you!"

Natalie gave the man her $850 and handed John an extra $200 for his portion. Once they were all paid, they headed back out to the car to get the bags. John could tell that Natalie was upset, so he grabbed her bag too. With bags in hand, the couple headed upstairs to their room. Once they arrived, they could see the gorgeous view right off the boardwalk! Natalie was speechless. This was one of the most beautiful things she had ever seen. She looked back and gave John a smile as he headed inside with their bags.

Once Natalie was done admiring the view for the time being, she headed into the room to help John unpack the bags. The room wasn't quite what she was expecting, but she wasn't expecting to be inside much. John apologized to Natalie again for needing the money, and Natalie said, "John, it's not about the money. It's about you not even telling me you needed extra money until we are at the desk, and I have no choice in the matter. But I would really like to just forget about it and have a good time with you, okay?"

John agreed that was for the best, and they finished unpacking.

As they were putting clothes away in their drawers, Natalie came across her bikini and towel. She looked at John and with excitement in her voice exclaimed, "Let's go to the beach!"

A little startled, John agreed! He told Natalie he had never been to a beach before or in the ocean, so he was a little nervous. Natalie hugged him and said everything would be okay. They would take things as slow as he needed.

After the two had changed into their bathing suits, they grabbed their room key and headed down the steps to the beach. They were so excited, giggling and holding hands all the way down the steps onto the boardwalk. Natalie greeted the lifeguard on the beach, and they showed him their passes, and he waved them in. That first step felt magical, squeezing the hot sand between their toes. As they got closer to the water, they set down their towels and headed toward the water.

"Don't go too deep now, John."

"I won't, babe. I just want to feel the water on my legs."

The waves felt so relaxing to both of them, and John spotted something shiny in the distance. It was a seashell that had been washed ashore by the waves. John yelled at Natalie that they should go seashell hunting, and she agreed that sounded really fun! For about thirty minutes and twenty seashells later, the two had the best time ever.

"Babe, I'm going to sit on my towel," Natalie told John.

"Okay, hun, just a little bit longer. I'm having too much fun!"

"Okay, hun, take your time. Then we can dry off and get something to eat."

Ten minutes later, John decided it was time to get out of the water and time to eat. When John went over to lay on his towel, Natalie asked him what he wanted to eat. John said he didn't care, but really, he was very picky about his food. So Natalie said since they were on the beach, this seemed like the perfect opportunity for fresh seafood! John agreed, and the two started to dry off and head back to the boardwalk.

As they were approaching the boardwalk, the couple took this opportunity to check out what restaurants were available. They saw a cute little restaurant about halfway down the boardwalk that looked perfect for their first night! Natalie pointed it out and asked John if that was okay. He excitedly replied yes, and the two headed on up to their room to change for dinner. On the way up the stairs, Natalie told John how happy she was to be here with him, hoping to smooth everything over from before. He smiled and said, "Me too, hun!"

Once at their room, Natalie took out the room key and opened the door. This was still an old-fashioned hotel with actual keys and not key cards for the door, so it took her a second. Once inside, the two ran to the closets and picked out their outfits for their first dinner of vacation together! Natalie chose a nice sundress to wear while John chose shorts and a tank top.

"Time to go!" John said.

And the couple headed back down to the boardwalk together in complete bliss.

Since the hotel was right on the boardwalk, there were a lot of games, concession stands, restaurants, and oh ya, more games! As the two walked down the boardwalk, they could smell seafood and steak and burgers, everything just smelled so good! This only made Natalie hungrier, but John saw all of the games and wanted to play. Natalie hesitantly obliged. "But only for a few minutes, John. I'm really hungry."

"Okay, hun. They just look so fun! We don't have these back home."

A few minutes turned into an hour and a lot of quarters later.

"Okay, John. It's been an hour! I'm starving, and you promised only a few minutes!"

"I'm sorry, hun. You're right. But I have to run back to the room to grab some more money for dinner."

"Seriously, John? How much could you have possibly spent in there?"

"Too much. You stay here, hun. I'll be right back. Do you need anything from the room?"

"No, thanks. Just hurry please."

"You just go to the restaurant, and I'll meet you there."

"Are you sure?"

"Yes."

With that, Natalie headed to the restaurant alone, and John went back to the room. The restaurant was outdoor seating, so John would easily be able to find her. She sat down and ordered herself a drink to calm her nerves. Some time passed, and John never showed up. The waiter came back and asked, "Are you still waiting, or are you ready to order?"

Natalie hated to order without John, but she was just so hungry. "I'm ready, I'll have the swordfish please."

"Great choice! I'll be back shortly with that."

Frustrated, Natalie sent John a text, asking where in the world he was. Naturally there was no reply, and within a few minutes, her food arrived. Natalie finished up her swordfish and drink, paid, and walked back to the room distraught. DING, DING. It was John! He texted that she just walked past him on the boardwalk and asked where she was going. She was so upset, she put the phone back in her pocket and headed up to the room.

After arriving at the room, Natalie changed into her comfy clothes and turned the TV on. This was definitely not how she expected the very first day of their vacation to be. Natalie started to doze off to the sounds of the TV as John walked in.

"Hey, babe, I'm sorry about dinner. Why didn't you answer my text?"

"Why didn't you show up for dinner or answer my text? I sat there alone waiting for you like an idiot!"

"I'm sorry, Natalie. I went back to the room and got more money. As I was walking back to the restaurant to meet up with you, I saw a machine with the new iWatches in them and really wanted one. I guess I lost track of time."

"I don't want to hear it, John! I can't believe this is how the first day of vacation turned out! I want to go home!"

With this, John didn't know what to say, so he just turned around and left. By now Natalie was in tears. She turned the TV off and headed to bed. This fight would actually set the tone for the rest of vacation, and the two hardly even talked to each other and definitely didn't spend time together. Natalie thought this may have been the worst idea that she ever had. Instead of enjoying her time, Natalie was counting down the days until she could leave and be with her one true love again—Rufus. When that day finally came, there were no tears, there were no long faces, at least on her end, of having to leave; but there was excitement, like excitement she felt to get there, but this was excitement that her pain would actually be over.

Despite not wanting to, Natalie walked down to the front desk with John in complete silence. When they got to the front desk, the manager asked, "How was your stay? I hope it was everything you dreamed of!"

"We would just like to check out please."

"Okay, that's fine. May I have your beach passes back please?"

Natalie handed her pass back to the man, but John had lost his pass and didn't have the money to pay for it. When John asked Natalie for the money, her face actually turned red, and she said she would cover it, but they were going to have a serious talk on the way home. Just the pass was $50, so in total, she had to pay $1,100 for the worst week of her life!

John knew Natalie had hit her breaking point, so he told her he would pack the car, and she could just go sit in the car. There was no argument on her end because she figured that was the least he could do. Once the car was packed, they were headed back home. Once John got up the courage, he turned to Natalie and said, “I’m sorry about everything this week, Natalie.”

“I don’t want to hear it, John. You’re always sorry, but then you just continue to hurt me. Actions speak louder than words, and your actions let me know loud and clear that you aren’t sorry, and you don’t care about me.”

“Come on, Natalie. You know that’s not true.”

“No, John. I don’t know that. I’m sorry, but I can’t do this anymore. This week has shown me this is not what I want, and I cannot continue this way. I’m sorry, but we’re over!”

“No! You can’t mean that!”

“But I do. Can you please just not talk to me for the rest of the ride back?”

CHAPTER 9

Gone but Not for Long

AS NATALIE PULLED INTO John's driveway, she felt like her heart had fallen out of her chest. Oddly, she also felt a sort of content knowing that this was for the best. As John got his things out of the trunk, he begged Natalie to reconsider her decision to end things with him. He told her he knew he screwed up, but he was so sorry, and it would never happen again. As hard as it was, Natalie kept an emotionless face and just asked him to please go away. A tear rolled down his face as he took his things inside.

As soon as his front door shut, Natalie gave out a sigh of relief. It was finally over! She then headed to her mom's house to pick up her beloved Rufus. As she pulled in her mom's driveway, Natalie could see her mom and Rufus looking out the window, waiting for her. No sooner did she put the car into park that Rufus came running out the front door. The biggest smile came across her face, at least the biggest in the past week.

Rufus immediately jumped in the car. He was ready to go home, and so was Natalie! But Natalie did have to get a lot off her chest with her mom first. Natalie motioned for Rufus to go back into the house, and he clumsily obliged. An immediate concern came across Rebecca's face as she walked with her daughter inside the house.

As soon as Rebecca closed the door, it was like the floodgates had opened up. Natalie immediately broke down, collapsing on the couch. Rebecca immediately grabbed the box of tissues and came to her daughter's need.

"What's wrong, baby? You should be so happy right now."

"I know, Mom, but instead, I'm completely devastated and have no clue what to do now."

"What do you mean? What happened? Wasn't vacation great?"

"Vacation was a mistake, John was a mistake, and now I have no one and no job."

"Don't be ridiculous, baby. You'll always have me. Wipe those tears away now, and tell me what happened."

"I don't want to talk about it, Mom. I just want to forget. Forget it and forget him!"

"Do you mean you two broke up?"

"Yes, Mom, okay? Yes—is that what you want to hear?"

"Oh, baby, of course it's not what I want to hear. I want you to be happy and successful. We will figure out what to do from here."

"Thanks, Mom. I really appreciate it. I love you!"

"I love you, too, baby girl!"

With a hug and a kiss, Natalie gathered Rufus, thanked her mom for everything, and headed to the car. Rufus immediately climbed into the passenger seat and gave Natalie a big wet kiss. She smiled, laughed, and said, "Let's go home, buddy!"

As Natalie was driving home, her phone kept going off. She didn't even care to look because she knew who it was and what he wanted. Once she pulled into her driveway and parked the car, she let Rufus out. He was so happy to be home that he ran to the front door and waited to be left in. Natalie opened the door to let him in and went back to the car to get the bags. Thank God she didn't have many bags because she was mentally and emotionally drained from everything that had gone on in the past week.

Once all the bags were in the house, she closed the front door, poured herself a glass of wine, and sat on the couch with Rufus. "I sure hope your week was better than mine, buddy."

Rufus just looked at her with those puppy-dog eyes and laid down on her lap. She knew it was a bad idea, but she decided to look at her phone to see what John could possibly have to say to her.

Much to her surprise, he didn't say anything; it was actually a video. The video was pictures of all of their time together, from when they first started dating and even a few from the vacation. To make it even sweeter, the video had a song—their song—that really tugged at her heartstrings. Natalie was crying again, and she didn't know why.

This didn't change what he did or how he acted, but this was the first time he really proved he cared about her. She felt like her mind was going in a million different directions, and she didn't know how to feel about anything. Natalie sat in silence for a while with Rufus as she sipped on her glass of wine. Just as she finished her last sip, the doorbell rang.

CHAPTER 10

He Can Change

IT WAS JOHN WITH a single red rose, just like he gave her on their first date. Her heart sank, and her face was completely flush.

"What do you want, John?"

"Look, I know you're mad at me, and I deserve it. I just came by to check on you and see if you were okay."

"Are you kidding me? Of course, I'm not okay, John. Did you think a few pictures and a song was going to make up for everything?"

"Of course not, babe, but I was hoping you might give me a chance to explain everything to you. Can I come in?"

Hesitantly, Natalie opened the door and motioned him in. Naturally Rufus was excited to see him again and jumped up and gave him a kiss. John laughed and sat down on the couch with him. Natalie didn't want to, but she gave a slight smirk, closed the door, and sat down on the couch.

"John, what could we possibly have to talk about at this point?"

"Listen, Natalie, I'm so sorry about everything. Please, please, please give me another chance! You are the best thing that has ever happened to me, and I will spend the rest of my life trying to make things right with you!"

"I don't know, John. I gave up everything for you, and it just seems like you couldn't care less."

"That's not true. I care more than you know! Please! How about we go to the arcade tomorrow? You love the arcade, and I will pay for everything!"

"I guess there's no harm in that. What time?"

"Let's go about noon tomorrow. That way, we have plenty of time to do whatever you want."

"Okay, John, but this is your last chance."

"Okay, hun, thank you! I love you!"

"I love you too, but I really don't like you right now."

"That's fair. So I'm not going to try and kiss you tonight, I'll give you your space, and I'll just see you tomorrow."

"Thank you. Good night."

"Good night, baby."

As Natalie got ready for bed, she was so confused. She loved John, but she was just so mad at him right now and didn't know if she could do this her whole life. As she reached over to turn out the lights, there was just one question in her mind—was he worth it?

The next morning was the day they were going to the arcade together. Natalie didn't want to admit it to herself, but she was really excited. This place they were going had cosmic mini golf, bowling, laser tag, bumper cars, games, and a mini racetrack!

It was twelve o'clock on the dot, and the doorbell rang. It was John standing there with a smile on his face and tickets in his hand.

"Are you ready to have a great time, babe?"

"Yes, I am! I'm really excited for this!"

"Me too, babe. Come on!"

Natalie said goodbye to Rufus and locked the door behind her. The arcade was only a fifteen-minute drive away, so they weren't stuck in the car long. As they pulled into the packed parking lot, they both felt a sense of relief fall over them. This could be the start of a new beginning for them. They shut the car doors and headed inside.

After giving the lady at the front desk their tickets, Natalie headed straight for the race cars. John laughed and chased after her, telling her to wait up! Standing in line for the race track, John turned to her and pointed. "What's that over there?" Natalie looked but didn't see anything and turned back around to find him on one knee and a ring!

"Natalie, after everything we have been through, especially this past week, I have realized you are the one for me, and I never want to lose you. Just like this racetrack, I want to show you that I will always win the race to your heart. Will you marry me?"

Natalie stood speechless with her mouth wide open and everyone staring at her. She could not believe what just happened—was she dreaming? After a few seconds, which seemed like an eternity of being put on the spot, she said, "Yes, John, I will marry you!"

And just like in a movie, everyone cheered as John put the ring on her finger and kissed her.

"Now it really is you and me against the world forever!" he said.

CHAPTER 11

Paralyzing Defeat

JOHN AND NATALIE HAD a wonderful time at the arcade together. It was the best time Natalie had in a while. On the ride home, Natalie couldn't stop smiling and looking at her ring.

"Do you like it, babe?" John asked.

"Oh, yes! You did such a good job!"

"You deserve so much more, but it's all I had right now."

"Don't be silly, hun. It's perfect!" she told him.

"I'm so glad you like it. We are going to be so happy together, babe!"

Natalie wasn't sure why, but she had this empty, nagging feeling in the pit of her stomach. Was she doing the right thing? She was with him for so long, but times like vacation just couldn't be forgotten. Maybe he realized what he had and would change. Maybe everything would be okay, and she was just overreacting. Either way, she was pretty sure this was not how total bliss right after an engagement was supposed to feel.

When John dropped her back off at the house, he gave her a kiss and told her how much he loved her. He asked if she wanted him to stay the night, but Natalie was still unsure how she felt about everything so made up an excuse of why he couldn't. John smiled and nodded his head as Natalie turned around to walk inside the house.

Just as Natalie put her key in the door, her phone went off with a text message. She turned around to see if maybe it was John, but he was already gone. She ignored the phone until she got inside.

Naturally Rufus was waiting in the hallway to greet her with his big goofy grin. "Hey, boy! Did you miss me?"

His tail wagged as he jumped about. "Who wants to go outside?"

Rufus gave a bark and ran to the back door for Natalie to let him out.

Once Rufus was outside, Natalie looked at her phone. It was a text from an unknown number that read, "You're in danger!" Natalie was so confused. Was this a joke? It had to be a joke from one of her friends or something.

So she wrote back, "Ha ha, very funny. Who is this?"

"Please listen to me before it's too late. This is not a joke. I'm trying to help you!"

"Who is this?" she asked again.

"My name isn't really important, but I needed to warn you about John."

Now Natalie was very interested. "How do you know me or my fiancé?"

"Because he used to be my fiancé and was just at my place a few days ago in my bed."

"WHAT! That's not possible!" she exclaimed.

"Why, because you're so in love, and he wants to do everything with you? Please just listen to me, even if you don't believe me."

At this point, Natalie's face went completely white, and she felt like she was going to throw up. *This couldn't be true*, she thought. *He loves me and wants to marry me!*

"I am so sorry to have to do this to you, Natalie. I really am, but you deserve to know the truth before you marry this guy."

"Wait, he just proposed to me. How did you know?"

"Because I work at the arcade. The one he takes all the girls to in order to run his scam on them. And that ring of yours, I actually bought that when he said he wanted to marry me."

"No, that can't be true. We have a deep connection. We just got back from—"

"Vacation? Where he told you he had never been to the beach to make you feel closer to him? You don't have to believe a word that I say, but maybe you will believe your own eyes."

Suddenly a flood of pictures started coming through, showing John and some girl together. Pictures at the arcade, beach, movies, mini golf, etc.

"I'm so sorry, Natalie, but you needed to know. And we aren't the only two. I actually hired a private investigator after we broke up, and he has been running this scam all across the country! He makes women feel special and loved, but really, he just wants their money and them to support him. John is not capable of love."

At this, Natalie fell to her knees and started sobbing uncontrollably. She wanted the universe to swallow her whole at that very moment just so she wouldn't have to feel this way. Natalie crawled over to the phone and called her mother. When Rebecca answered, the only words Natalie could get out were, "Mom, come over."

Rebecca was in such shock. She said, "Absolutely, baby, I'm on my way!"

When Rebecca got over to her daughter's house, the door was unlocked, so she just let herself in. Still having no idea what to expect, Rebecca was in mommy-panic mode. When she found her daughter in a ball on the floor, Rebecca dropped her purse and keys and ran to her side.

"Baby, oh my gosh, what's wrong!?!"

"It's J…J…it's John." She sobbed.

"What about John? Come on, let's get you on the couch. Where's Rufus?"

"Oh, I forgot, he's outside. Let him in please, Mom."

"Of course, baby."

Once Rufus was in, he came to console his mamma on the couch immediately.

"Get down, buddy. I'll help your mamma. Now what happened, Natalie? What about John?"

"He's a complete monster, Mom. He was playing me this whole time. He even asked me to marry him, see."

"Oh my gosh, after that vacation you guys just had? I thought you were going to break up."

"So did I, but then he took me to the arcade and proposed to me in the sweetest way. But apparently, he's been doing this all over the country!"

"WHAT! Baby, I'm so sorry. How did you find out?"

"After the arcade, I received a text from an unknown number, and a woman told me everything!"

"Baby, how do you know she wasn't lying?"

"There were pictures and an actual police report, Mom!"

At this, Rebecca didn't know what to say. The two just sat there in complete silence while she held her daughter.

CHAPTER 12

Don't Let the Door Hit You on the Way Out!

REBECCA AND HER DAUGHTER were still sitting on the couch completely speechless when Rebecca said, "You need to confront him now, Natalie."

There was surprisingly no argument from Natalie, just a simple, "How?"

Rebecca just shook her head, gave her daughter a kiss on the forehead, and headed out the door.

This was something Natalie had to take care of on her own, and she couldn't act like it never happened. Her voice was still too shaky to talk, so she sent John a text, saying, "Come over now please."

A few seconds went by, and he replied, "Okay."

Natalie was starting to sweat, thinking about what she was going to say to someone who was supposed to love her but now didn't know if he even liked her.

Ten minutes went by, and there was a knock on her front door. Natalie rushed Rufus into her bedroom so they could talk without being interrupted. When Natalie opened the door and saw John, a sudden irrefutable anger came over her. When he leaned in to kiss her, she turned her head and pulled away.

"Is everything okay, babe?"

"Come sit down please. We need to talk about something."

With a confused look, he came in and walked over to sit down on the couch. "Where's Rufus? Why is it so quiet in here? Are you okay, Natalie?"

"No, John, no, I'm not. I received some very disturbing news."

"Okay?" he said, still trying to play it cool. "About what?"

"About you, John. You and you're, let's say, history."

"What are you talking about, Natalie?"

"Please just stop the games. You know exactly what I am talking about. So how many were there? How many women did you play this whole charade with before me?"

"What? You're crazy!"

"And you're caught. I've seen the pictures. I've seen the police report. The only thing I can't figure out is why? Why me, John?"

"Natalie, I love you! Please stop this nonsense!"

"Nonsense? How many women across the country have you proposed to before me, John? How many women did you make feel special, all just to get what you want?"

"Baby, so I made mistakes, but I never played anyone. Please believe me! Don't do this to us!"

"I'm not doing anything, John. I just finally opened my eyes."

Knowing he was caught, John started to give a smirk of satisfaction. "Okay, you're right. And you know what? It was easy! You women are so desperate for love and acceptance, you don't see what is going on right in front of your very eyes."

"GET OUT! GET OUT OF MY HOUSE AND MY LIFE!"

John turned around to walk away but not without saying, "You'll be back. They all come back."

ABOUT THE AUTHOR

JESSICA CONSIDERS HERSELF TO be a pretty laid back, happy-go-lucky person, but unfortunately, she has managed to get herself into some difficult situations. Thankfully, she was able to work past them and make them into these wonderful books!

To anyone reading this, she wants you to know that you are not alone, and there is always help out there if you ask. Don't be ashamed, and definitely don't feel like something is your fault just because you were in a bad situation. Always remember, coming out of a terrible situation doesn't make you a victim; it makes you a survivor!

As a new author, Jessica is very excited to share her experiences and thoughts with the world. She hopes that she would eventually be able to reach enough people in order to really help someone—even just a family member or a friend—in their own life. Writing has always been a passion of hers, and she hopes she has the opportunity to continue to share her writing with everyone who wishes to read it!

CPSIA information can be obtained
at www.ICGtesting.com
Printed in the USA
BVHW060351310821
615173BV00004B/81

9 781098 09980